Ruth Sil

The Old
Who Lived In A
ROUNDABOUT

"A roundabout," he whispered. "It's a roundabout."

He looked at the animals with their twisting brass poles. There was no mistake. It was a real, old, roundabout. But what was it doing there? There were weeds and grass growing all round it and it looked a bit lop-sided too. It must have been there for years and years, thought Joe.

Other titles in the STREAMERS series:

Ruth Silvestre

The Old Woman
Who Lived In A
ROUNDABOUT

Illustrated by Caroline Ewan

Hippo Books
Scholastic Publications Limited
London

Scholastic Publications Ltd.,
10 Earlham Street, London WC2H 9RX, UK

Scholastic Inc.,
730 Broadway, New York, NY 10003, USA

Scholastic Tab Publications Ltd.,
123 Newkirk Road, Richmond Hill,
Ontario L4C 3G5, Canada

Ashton Scholastic Pty Ltd.,
P O Box 579, Gosford, New South Wales,
Australia

Ashton Scholastic Ltd.,
165 Marua Road, Panmure, Auckland 6,
New Zealand

First published by Scholastic Publications Ltd., 1991
Illustration copyright © Caroline Ewan

ISBN 0 590 76413 6

Printed by Cox & Wyman Ltd, Reading, Berks

Chapter One

It was Saturday morning and Joe was just going out. Joe always went exploring on Saturdays. His father had a café called TONI'S. Joe's mother worked there and his Auntie Nina, and Saturday was their busiest day. It was Joe's day to go exploring.

Fixed to his belt Joe had a

compass, a plastic water bottle and a purse with 10p in it. This was for the telephone in case he ever got lost. He never had. His father had shown him where his road was on the street map. Joe loved maps. He had them pinned all over his bedroom.

Joe locked the door carefully and dropped the keys through the letter box. He walked down the steps. It was summer and the sun was warm. He sniffed the air. It smelled good. Next door's tree was covered in white flowers. The branches hung over the pavement. As he walked underneath Joe looked up and took a big sniff. Wow! They smelled as strong as Auntie Nina's scent. He felt the whole world was a little bit crazy today. It was just the day for an adventure.

He waited for the green man so that he could cross the road safely, then he strode on. He jumped on all the low walls, balancing along them with his arms out, like an aeroplane. In the gutter he found an old tin. He kicked it in front of him all along the pavement. It made a wonderful din, Bingle, Bangle, Bong! He stroked a ginger cat that was lying on the wall. Its fur was warm from the sun and it rolled over and purred like an engine.

Joe walked on and on. He felt bursting with energy. He looked at everything. How interesting the world was. When he was grown up he would explore every bit of it. He turned another corner and suddenly realized he'd never been down this road before. Good, he thought, now I'm really exploring.

There were houses on one side of the road and a high hedge on the other. It was full of spiders' webs. Joe picked a long piece of grass and poked it gently into the edge of a web. He shook the web and waited.

A fat spider came dashing out to see if he'd caught a fly. Joe laughed. "Got you that time!" he said.

The houses stopped and the road

grew narrower. It was a bit muddy and seemed to be coming to an end. But Joe could see a path. He pushed his way through the tall weeds. He trod down the stinging nettles and smelled their bitter smell. The path climbed a slope and halfway up Joe stopped. In the distance, through the bushes, he could just see something. It was coloured and large and round. Joe was amazed. For a moment he stood quite still. Then he began to run, pushing his way through. He could hardly believe his eyes.

"A roundabout," he whispered. "It's a roundabout."

He looked at the animals with their twisting brass poles. There was no mistake. It was a real, old,

roundabout. But what was it doing there? There were weeds and grass growing all round it and it looked a bit lop-sided too. It must have been there for years and years, thought Joe. He went slowly towards it. He was very excited. In all his exploring he had never discovered anything like this. He went closer until he could look up at one of the great animals. It was a horse, black with staring eyes. The one behind it was white with spots and the next one looked as though it might have been a zebra but the stripes were almost worn away.

Next to the spotted horse was a big bird. Joe supposed it was an ostrich. Then he saw a giraffe and a dragon which was so long that there were three seats on its back. Each animal had a twisting golden pole through the middle which fixed it to the floor and to the painted top. All round the edge of the roof were faded letters. It was hard to read them because the paint was peeling off.

Joe began to walk right round.

ANIMAL GALLOPERS

"Animal what?" said Joe aloud. He was just about to start round again when a door in the middle of the roundabout flew open and a head popped out.

Chapter Two

Joe stood quite still. He stared into
the blackest yet brightest eyes that he
had ever seen. The head came
further out until he could see the
whole person. It was a very small,
very old woman. She was all
wrapped in brown like a faded leaf.
She wore wellington boots with the
tops rolled over and on her head she
had a man's cap. This almost made
Joe laugh but there was something
about this old woman that stopped
him. She slipped between the
animals and stepped down, peering
at him closely.

"And who are you?" she asked.
Her voice was thin but sharp.

Joe looked at her. "I'm not
supposed to talk to strangers," he said.

"Please yourself," she answered.
Then, "Quite right!"

They looked at one another.

She can't be very dangerous,
thought Joe. She's really old and
she's not much bigger than I am. He
wondered if he ought to shake hands

and decided that he'd better.

"I'm Joe," he said as he held out his hand. The old woman smiled. She had a tooth missing at the front just like Joe'd had when he first started school. But he'd grown a new one a long time ago.

The smile made the old woman's brown face go into lots of creases and her black eyes almost disappeared. She took Joe's hand in hers and shook it gently. Then she turned it over and looked into his palm.

"You'll have a long life, my dear," she said softly. "A long life. See, there it is. In your hand." With her brown finger she traced a line across his palm and down to his wrist. It tickled. She looked up at him. "And what's more, my dear," she said, "you're going to do a lot of travelling, yes, a lot of travelling."

Joe was pleased. She was clever to know that, this funny old woman.

"That's because I'm going to be an explorer," he said. "I'm going all over the world."

"I see." She nodded. She still held his hand and looked at him with those black eyes. "Maybe you will," she said, "maybe you will."

Her hand was very small and dry as paper. Joe pulled his own hand gently away. "Is this your roundabout?" he asked. "What's it doing here?"

"What's it doing here?" repeated the old woman. "It's not doing anything. It's like me, too old to work and too tired to go travelling. It's my home. I live in it and," she waved her arm, "I have all my friends round me. What could be better than that, eh?"

"Nothing," said Joe. He didn't know what else to say.

She climbed back onto the roundabout and Joe followed. "This is Dukie," she said, patting the spotted horse, "and this is Georgie, the giraffe." She laughed a little wheezy laugh. "He's got such a long neck he easily gets a sore throat. I have to remember to put his scarf on when the weather gets cold." She turned suddenly and looked at Joe with her head on one side. She's dotty, thought Joe, nice but dotty.

"Would you like a cup of tea?" she

asked him.

"Er—yes please." Joe wasn't very keen on tea but it seemed the only thing to say.

"This way, then." The old woman stepped between the animals and disappeared through the narrow doorway into the middle of the roundabout. Joe followed.

He found himself in the most fantastic home that he had ever seen. To begin with, it was, as you might expect, round. In the middle was all the machinery which worked the roundabout with something hanging on every knob and handle. There were bags and baskets, saucepans and bits of cloth. Joe saw a knife and fork on a string, a dusty mirror, a pair of slippers and some big, black

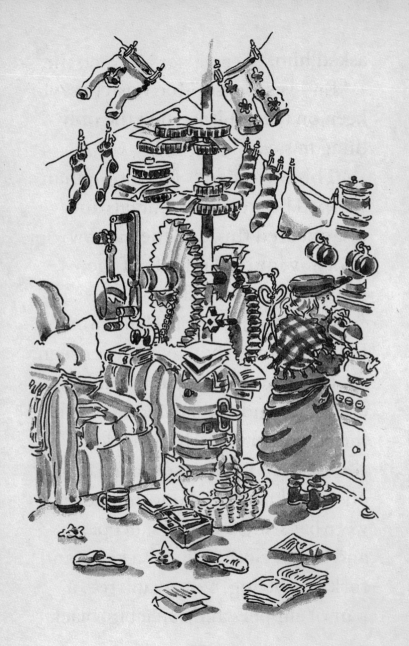

16

scissors. In every space between the wheels and cogs were papers and old letters. Above his head were lines with more things hanging from them. Every part of this strange, round room was crammed full.

The old woman filled a kettle from a jug and put a flame to a tiny stove. "Now, let me see," she said, "what about a biscuit? Boys like biscuits." She reached down a tin.

"Yes. Yes, please," murmured Joe, still gazing round this strangest of strange homes. He walked slowly round the machinery until he came back to where the old woman was pouring the water into a teapot. "You haven't got a bed," he said.

"Quite right," she answered, unhooking two cups from the wall.

Joe was puzzled. "But where do you sleep then?"

She chuckled. "Bless me, why, in my comfy old chair, of course. When you get to be as old as me you don't need so much sleep." She looked at Joe. "I'm not growing like you are, you know. I'm shrinking more like." She laughed. "And anyway," she went on, "tis a pity to waste all the night hours. I like to watch the moon and the stars, and when it's not too cold I wait for my night friends."

"Your night friends?" Joe did not understand.

"Hedgehogs, they're my night friends. Hotchiwitchis we used to call them when I was a girl."

Joe laughed. "Hotchiwitchis!" he said. "That's a funny word."

"It's a gypsy name," said the old woman. "It's not English."

"My granny's not English," said Joe. "She's Italian. So's my dad and my Auntie Nina. My granny's gone back to Italy," he added sadly. "She used to live with us but the cold in England got into her bones, so she went back."

"My bones are used to the cold," said the old woman, pouring the tea into cups. They took them outside and sat down on the edge of the roundabout in the sun. Joe munched his biscuit.

"Yes," said the old woman, pointing. "Under them bricks, that's where they've got their nest, my hedgehogs. See that little space? That's where they come strolling

19

out, snuffling along to see what they can find. They just enjoy a drop of bread and milk." She smiled. "And sometimes I get another visitor."

"Who?" asked Joe.

"The old fox," she answered. "He likes an egg, does the old fox. He'll come right up and take it from my hand. So, you see, it wouldn't do to be fast asleep when my visitors come a-calling, would it now?"

"No," said Joe. He looked at her. She was a really funny old woman but he liked her. "Have you always lived here in the roundabout?" he asked.

"Oh, no," she laughed and hugged her knees. "Why, when I was your age—how old are you?"

"Seven and three quarters," said Joe, "nearly eight."

"Very nice," she said. "Well—I lived in a waggon then with my two brothers. Travellers we were. Always going somewhere different."

"That sounds great," said Joe. "Like exploring, really."

"I suppose it was." The old woman smiled. "We made clothes pegs and

21

come Springtime we'd pick flowers and tie them in bunches to sell."

"Didn't you go to school, then?" asked Joe.

She grinned at him. "Once or twice, when we stayed somewhere for a few weeks."

"Crikey!" said Joe. "I have to go every day—except weekends, of course, and holidays."

"Things were different in them days," said the old woman. "We didn't go to school much but we learned a lot of other things. Always busy, we were, and when we ran home the fire would be crackling and my mother would have something good cooking in a big pot." She sighed, smiling to herself. She stopped talking and closed her eyes. Joe hoped she wasn't going to fall asleep.

"And the roundabout?" he asked. "What about the roundabout?"

The old woman opened her eyes and looked at him as though she had forgotten he was there.

"Oh, the roundabout," she said, "that belonged to my husband. He died a long, long time ago. Every summer we'd take it all over the country. Hundreds of children riding the animals." She smiled. "Then, when it got too cold, we'd find somewhere to rest up, like here." She nodded. "Then when Spring came round we'd paint it up—smart—and off we'd go again."

"That sounds great," said Joe.

"Yes, it was." The old woman

smiled at him. Then she got up and patted the spotted horse. "But we're too old now, aren't we, Dukie-boy? We stay here and look after each other." She turned suddenly. "I'm tired now. I'm off for a nap. What did you say your name was?"

"Joe," he called, watching her slide through the narrow door into the roundabout. "What's yours?"

"Granny Peg, they call me," she said, and the door closed.

Joe walked home thinking about Granny Peg and her roundabout. How wonderful it would be to go exploring all summer. On and on, somewhere new every day. That would just suit him.

He walked until he came to his dad's café. He pushed the door open. It smelled good and, as usual, was very busy. "Good Italian food. Sensible prices. They always come back." That's what his dad said. Joe's mother came out of the kitchen

carrying lots of plates all up her arm. She was very good at that. She smiled at him.

"Hello, Joe. Go and have your dinner. You're a bit late today."

"I've been exploring," said Joe. "I've found the most fantastic . . ."

"Yes, yes, later, Joe." His mother put down the plates and hurried to the next table with her pad and pencil on a string. She began to write down the orders.

Joe sighed and went through to the kitchen where his Auntie Nina was washing up. She dried her hands on her apron and served him a big bowl of spaghetti with loads of sauce. He didn't even bother to tell her or his father about his adventure. His father was so busy, chopping, then stirring and the fan in the kitchen made such a lot of noise that he probably wouldn't hear him anyway. His father grinned at him over a cloud of steam.

"You OK, Joe?" he shouted.

"OK," called Joe. He curled the spaghetti round his fork and slid it into his mouth. He was really hungry. He began to wonder if it had all been a dream. An old woman living in a roundabout? Who would believe that?

Chapter Three

On Sundays the café was closed.
Joe's father always stayed in bed late
and Joe's mother cooked the dinner.
"English food on Sundays," she
would say. "Roast beef and
Yorkshire pudding and apple pie, eh
Joe?"

Joe didn't much care what he ate.
When his granny had lived with
them she had always cooked on
Sundays.

Joe wished she hadn't gone back to
Italy. She had always had time to talk
to him. He could have told her about

the old woman in the roundabout.
When she started to get pains in her
back and her legs the doctor said she
needed the sun. So she went back to
Italy. Now all Joe got were postcards.
He had them all pinned up under
his maps. It looked lovely in Italy.
He wished they could go there but
his dad said they would have to wait
until the café was making more
money.

   After they had all had their
dinner, it was Joe's mother's turn for
a rest. She took off her apron, hung
it on the back of the kitchen door
and said "That's me!" She put her
feet up on the sofa and began to
watch the television. Joe knew that in
ten minutes she would be fast asleep.

   Joe got out the street map of his

town. He opened it on the floor. First he found his own road. Then he tried to remember which way he had gone yesterday. How many corners had he turned? He traced it with his finger. No. That couldn't be the way. That road came out on the big, main road. He went back to his own road and began again.

"What are you doing, Joe?" his father asked.

"I'm trying to find where I went yesterday," he said.

His father came and sat on the floor beside him.

"I went down there," said Joe, pointing on the map, "across the main road—"

"At the crossing?" asked his father.

"Of course," sighed Joe. "Then I walked down that street. You see. BERRY STREET. I remember the name. Then I turned by the letter box and then—oh blow, I can't find it."

"What exactly are you looking for?" asked his father, yawning.

"A road that doesn't go anywhere really," said Joe.

"Doesn't sound very interesting to me." Joe's father stretched out on the floor and closed his eyes.

"It was! It was!" cried Joe. "It started as an ordinary road but then it got narrower and narrower and then there was a roundabout."

His father opened one eye and looked at him. "A roundabout?"

"Yes," said Joe.

"At the end of a road going nowhere?" His father opened his other eye.

"Yes!" cried Joe. "And there was an old woman living in the middle of the roundabout."

"JOE!" His father sighed. "I thought you'd grown out of all that. You remember the crocodile you saw in someone's front garden? And the time you told us you'd seen a space ship landing?"

"I know, I know!" shouted Joe. "I was only small then. Now I'm nearly eight. She's real, I tell you. I knew you wouldn't believe me. I knew it!"

Joe's father reached into his pocket. "Here," he said, "here's 50p. Go get an ice cream, Joe, and calm down, eh? I'm tired."

When Joe went to bed that night he lay thinking about his adventure. He got out of bed. There was a big, shining moon. He wondered if Granny Peg was putting out bread and milk for her friends. What had she called them? Hotchiwitchis, that was it. He smiled as he remembered the funny name. And the old fox! Fancy giving him an egg. He got back into bed and moved his pillow so that he could still see the moon. I shall go and see her again next Saturday, he thought as he fell asleep.

Chapter Four

Next Saturday when Joe got up it
was raining but by the time he had
finished his breakfast it had stopped.
Joe was pleased. His father had
already gone to work. Saturday
night was the busiest night at the café.

Joe got his things ready to go
exploring. As he was filling his water
bottle his mother came in the back
door. She had been pegging some
washing on the line. "It's going to be
a fine day after all," she said. "Look,
Joe, all those clouds are blowing
away."

"I'm glad," said Joe. "I'm going exploring."

"Mind you don't go too far," said his mother. "I worry about you, Joe." The phone rang and she ran to answer it. "Yes. Yes, I'm coming!" she shouted and she banged the phone down again. "Your father!" she said. "He thinks I've got ten pairs of hands. Lock up carefully, Joe."

"Yes, Mum," said Joe.

"And wear your watch," she said, putting on her coat.

"Yes, Mum."

"And come for your dinner as soon as you're hungry."

"Yes, Mum!" She kissed him and ran out of the house.

Joe was a bit worried in case he

couldn't find the way to the roundabout. Once he was across the main road and into Berry Street he looked about him very carefully. Yes, he was quite sure he had walked past this turning and the next one and—he stood on the corner. Was it here he had turned? Suddenly he noticed a house with a swing in the garden. Yes, he remembered that. Good. He ran on. He crossed over and hurried down the next street. Yes. He was excited now. The road to the roundabout was round the next corner. There it was. The name was almost hidden in the hedge. WILLOW ROAD. Good, now he'd be able to look it up on the street map and mark it with a felt tip. He might just show it to his dad.

Crocodiles! Didn't dad know that he'd grown up? He would be eight soon and going up into the Juniors.

He raced down the road, past where the houses stopped. The spiders' webs were still full of rain drops. They sparkled in the sunshine. But Joe didn't have time for them. He ran up the sloping path, then slowed down. Yes, there it was. He could see the top of the roundabout clearly over the bushes. He was so glad it hadn't been a dream.

When he pushed his way through the bushes he could see Granny Peg. She had been doing some washing just like his mum. Except that she didn't have a machine. She had a big bowl of soapy water on top of an old

box, and she had already pegged a few things on a line. She looked exactly the same except for a long, striped apron which came almost down to her feet. He watched her wring out a towel and spread it on a bush to dry. She hadn't heard him coming but the moment he stepped nearer she looked up. For a minute she looked quite cross, then she smiled.

"Oh, it's you, Joe," she said. "Where have you been, then?"

"School," said Joe. "I told you I have to go to school."

"Quite right," said Granny Peg.

"Didn't you make your children go to school?" asked Joe.

Granny Peg looked sad. "I never had any children, Joe," she said.

"Then how can you be a granny?"

"I'm not a real granny. It's just what they called me—all those children who used to ride the roundabout."

"Oh, I see," said Joe.

"As a matter of fact, I've no-one now in the whole world," she said.

"You have!" cried Joe. "You've got

40

the hedgehogs and the fox."

"Of course I have." She smiled.
"Cup of tea, Joe?" she asked as she
poured away the washing water. Joe
nodded. He didn't really want a cup
of tea but he did want another look
inside the roundabout. "You'll have
to go and get some water," she said.
"I've used it all up for the washing."

"Where do I get it from?" asked
Joe, looking round.

Granny Peg handed him a plastic
water bottle. It was just like the one
on his belt but much bigger.

"Follow that path," she said, "and
you'll find the tap."

Joe went the way she had pointed
and found a pipe sticking up out of
the ground with a tap on the top.
When he had filled the bottle it was

quite heavy and he had to carry it back slowly.

While Granny Peg boiled the kettle he had another look inside the roundabout.

"Whatever do you cut with this great big pair of scissors?" he asked. "They don't look very sharp."

"I bet if you was to go on guessing for a week you'd never know." Granny Peg smiled at him. "I don't use them. They belonged to my husband."

"Well, what did he cut, then?" asked Joe.

"Sweets."

"Sweets?" said Joe. "What kind of sweets?"

"The best sweets I ever tasted," said Granny Peg. "My husband used

to make them. He would boil up a
great pan of butter and sugar and
spices. Then he would pull up a long
strip like this. As it cooled he'd twist
it and then cut it with those great
scissors. I can tell you it smelled
wonderful."

"Mm," said Joe, "I love sweets."

"I wish I could give you a taste,
Joe, but nobody makes sweets like
that now."

"I wish they did," said Joe. He sat
down on the edge of Granny Peg's
comfy chair. "Did you sleep in this
chair when you were a little girl?" he
asked.

"Oh, no," said Granny Peg,
reaching down the biscuit tin. "I had
a nice bed in our waggon and my
brothers, they slept in a little tent.

Other kids used to shout 'Gypsy Gypsy live in a tent. Can't afford to pay the rent' but we didn't care. We didn't want to live in a house anyway. Here's your tea."

"I shall sleep in a tent when I grow up and go exploring," said Joe. He followed the old woman outside and they sat down on the edge of the roundabout.

It was a lovely morning. All the clouds had gone. Birds were singing in the bushes. Joe told Granny Peg all about his mother and father and the café. He told her how busy they always were and how he wished and wished that his granny hadn't gone back to Italy. Granny Peg listened. She sat very still, her head on one side. Suddenly she said, quietly, so quietly that Joe wasn't sure he'd heard her properly, "What about a ride? Eh, Joe?"

"A ride?" said Joe slowly, looking round. "Did you say a ride?"

Granny Peg nodded. Her black eyes were very bright.

"But—" said Joe, "does it still work—this roundabout?"

"Only for special people," she said, softly. "It all depends."

"Depends on what?"

"Whether you've got your head in the clouds or your feet on the ground." She laughed, the little rusty laugh he had heard before. Her small brown face creased up and her eyes glittered. Joe looked at her. She was dotty, quite dotty. He knew that and yet—there was something about her that he couldn't explain.

"Choose your seat!" she suddenly cried in a loud, clear voice. "CHOOSE YOUR SEAT PLEASE!"

Joe laughed. He climbed onto the back of Dukie, the spotted horse. "I'll choose this one!" he cried.

"And I'll ride the ostrich." The old woman climbed easily onto its back. She stretched out her arm. "Hold my hand for a minute," she said, "and shut your eyes and wish and wish and wish."

Joe closed his eyes and wished. For a moment nothing happened, then, suddenly, his heart seemed to float right out of his body. He heard— faintly at first and then louder— strange, old-fashioned music. Very

slowly, the old roundabout began to move. He felt the spotted horse rise up in the air, then slowly sink, and then rise up again. They were going round. The roundabout was turning and turning and turning. Faster and faster. He opened his eyes and looked at Granny Peg. She was hanging onto the golden pole with her head thrown back. Her long grey hair was flying out behind her in the wind and she was singing in a high piping voice.

Joe began to laugh. He closed his eyes again. The roundabout went faster and suddenly Dukie seemed to come alive beneath him. He felt its warmth and smelled its smell. It tossed its head and neighed with delight. "Faster! Faster!" yelled Joe.

And round and round they went. He felt as if they were soaring over the whole world. He felt as if he would burst with joy. What an adventure! What a ride!

At last, after what seemed like for ever, and yet no time at all, they began to slow down. Slower and slower they went. Joe felt his horse grow hard and wooden again. The music faded. They stopped. Joe opened his eyes. There were the trees and bushes and the washing out to dry. The birds were still singing and the sun still shining high in the sky. Joe looked at Granny Peg, very small and very still beside him on her scratched and peeling ostrich.

"Did it really happen?" he asked after a moment. "Did we really go

round and round and did the
animals . . .?"

The old woman leaned towards
him and put a papery finger on his
lips. "Ssh," she said softly. "You
mustn't talk about it. It's a secret. It
won't work for just anyone."

She climbed slowly down from the
ostrich's back and rubbed her hands
on her apron, yawning. "Now I'm
really tired," she said, smiling at Joe.
"I'm ready for forty winks in my
comfy old chair. But you must come
another day." She waved her hand
and disappeared into the
roundabout. The door banged shut
behind her.

Joe was alone. He slid off the
spotted horse. He walked slowly
down the steps. He looked back at

the roundabout. He saw the weeds
growing up through the floor. It
couldn't have gone round. It was
impossible and yet—it had. Joe knew
something very strange had
happened. This must be a magic
place, he thought.

He ran all the way back to the café
but by the time he got there he knew

he was not going to try telling anyone about anything. As he lay in bed that night, he thought over and over again about the wonderful ride and his dreams were filled with old-fashioned music and galloping horses.

Chapter Five

The next Friday as he walked home
from school, Joe was thinking about
the roundabout. He would go
tomorrow. He wondered if he would
get another ride. He hoped so. Then
he would really believe it had
happened.

There were only three more days
of school left before the summer
holidays began. It was very hot and
Joe was thirsty, so he walked round
the corner to the café. It was quiet;
there were only two customers
eating ice-cream. His father was

reading a newspaper. He got Joe some very cold orange juice from the kitchen.

"Where's Mum?" asked Joe.

His father looked gloomy. "She's round looking after your Auntie Nina," he said.

"Why? What's the matter with her?" asked Joe.

"She feels bad," said his father, "and the doctor says she must stay in bed for at least three days. I don't know how we're going to manage without her."

Joe could see that his father was really worried.

"What about me?" he asked. "I can help you, can't I?"

His father looked at him. "I suppose you could do a bit." He

smiled at Joe. "Yes. Why not?"

Joe was pleased that his father
needed him. I can go to the
roundabout another day. In the
holidays I can go any day I like, he
thought.

Joe's mother stuck her head round
the door. "I'm going to the chemist
to get some medicine," she called.

"I'll be back soon."

"I'm going to help you in the café. Dad says I can," said Joe, proudly.

His mother looked at him and smiled. "Good boy," she said. "You'd better start by giving us a hand this evening."

Joe had sometimes helped in the café before but only for fun. This time he felt really important. After he had eaten his own supper, Joe's father tied an apron around Joe's waist and gave him a pad and a pencil just like his mother's. She showed him how to write down the orders quickly. RAV for ravioli, SP for spaghetti, CH for chicken. Joe soon got the hang of it. He enjoyed it. The customers all smiled at him and they didn't seem to mind waiting

just a bit longer than usual. At first
his mother checked every order but
when she saw that he could manage
she left him on his own and dashed
backwards and forwards into the
kitchen.

When they paid the bill, the
customers left him money. At the
end of the evening, Joe had collected

nearly ten pounds. "Crikey!" he said. "I think I'll do this more often. I can save up to go to Italy."

"Oh, no, you won't. You're too young," said his father. "It's not allowed. This is just an emergency."

But he put his arm round Joe and hugged him and Joe felt happy. His legs ached and he was very tired. It was past eleven o'clock when he and his mother walked home.

"What time do we start tomorrow?" yawned Joe, as he pulled on his pyjamas.

"Ten o'clock," said his mother, "so you'd better go straight off to sleep."

Saturday was a really busy day. All the morning Joe rushed about with plates. Everyone seemed to be in a hurry. In the afternoon he fell asleep in a chair. The evening was the busiest time of all. On Sunday he understood why his father and mother were always so tired. Joe fell asleep in front of the television just like his mother.

Auntie Nina had the flu. She stayed in bed all that week. But on Saturday she was better and Joe did not need to help in the café. He was glad to have a day off. He would go exploring and see Granny Peg again. He was quite sure of the way now. He raced along Willow Road, past the spiders' webs, through the bushes until he reached the roundabout.

There was no sign of Granny Peg. It was very quiet. Joe walked round the roundabout. Then he walked

round again, whistling loudly. He
hoped she would come out. He
climbed the steps and stood outside
the narrow door. He knocked. He
waited. He knocked again. He felt
sure she was in there.

"Granny Peg!" he shouted. "It's
me. Joe."

He thought he heard a sound. It
could have been a cough. He called
again. Why wouldn't she come out?
He waited, looking at the door, but it
never opened.

Joe felt very sad. Why wouldn't
she open the door? He walked down
the steps. He went down the path to
the water tap and looked back.
There was no sign of her. Oh well,
he thought, if she won't come out
she won't. I suppose I might as well

go on exploring.

He walked on down the path. At
first it was very quiet but as he went
further he began to hear the noise of
cars and buses. At last he came to a
high fence, as high as a house. It had
a small door cut into it.

Joe opened the door, stepped
through and was surprised to find
himself in a busy street. On the other
side of the road were shops. I
suppose this is where Granny Peg
goes shopping, he thought. He
crossed the road carefully and
looked back at the high fence. It had
posters stuck all over it. You could
hardly see the door. No-one would
notice it, not unless they were
looking for it.

He crossed back again and slipped

through the door. I'll just have one more try at the roundabout, he said to himself. She might have been asleep in her old chair. But when he knocked and called there was still no reply. Joe walked home sadly. What if Granny Peg were ill? Perhaps she had the flu like his Auntie Nina. His dad said there was a lot of flu about. And Granny Peg had no-one in the world. She had told him so. He thought he'd heard her cough. Who would go to get her medicine?

When Joe lay in bed that night he couldn't sleep. He was really worried. He wanted to tell his mum and dad but he knew they wouldn't believe him.

Chapter Six

On Sunday afternoon Joe's father was reading the paper when he suddenly looked up. "Hey, Joe," he called. "It seems I was wrong."

"What about?" asked Joe.

"Your old roundabout," said his father. "Look, there's a picture of it in the paper."

Joe rushed to see. Sure enough, there was the roundabout amongst the trees and bushes. There was even a picture of Granny Peg as well.

"What does it say?" begged Joe, who could see that there were lots of long words. "Re-de-vel-op-ment." He spelled it out. "What does that mean?"

"It means," said his father, "that the Council have bought that bit of land and they're going to build there."

"But what about the roundabout and Granny Peg?" cried Joe.

Joe's father read a bit more. "It says here," he said, "that the Council have offered Mrs Peg a place in a home for old people on the other side of town but she doesn't want to move."

"Of course she doesn't!" shouted Joe. "She belongs in the roundabout. And what about all her friends?"

"What friends?" asked his father.

Joe told him about the hedgehogs and the fox. He didn't tell him about Dukie the spotted horse, or Georgie the giraffe, or the ride. Especially not the ride. He couldn't explain everything.

"It says here," said his father gently, "that Mrs Peg is eighty-four years old. That's very old, Joe. Much older than your granny in Italy. Perhaps she would be better off in a nice warm home. It must be cold living in a roundabout. Old people need a bit of looking after, you know.

"She's used to the cold. She told

me so," said Joe. Then he remembered. "Oh, Dad," he said, "when I went to see her yesterday she wouldn't come out. I think she might have the flu like Auntie Nina."

Joe looked so worried that his father folded up his paper and fetched his jacket. "Come on, Joe," he said. "You take me, eh? You show me your roundabout and we'll go and see the old lady. How's that?"

Joe was very pleased. His father never went out on Sundays, as a rule. Joe hopped along beside him, pointing out the way. Soon they came to the roundabout. Joe's father stood still for a moment and looked at it. "Just think how many children must have had a ride on that," he said softly.

Joe looked at his father. "Granny Peg can make magic, Dad."

"Can she?" His father smiled at him. "Well—there's not a lot of that about these days, I can tell you."

They walked up to the roundabout, hand in hand. Joe saw that the door was open just a crack.

"Granny Peg," he called, "it's Joe. Please come out. I've brought my dad to see you." There was no reply. "Granny Peg," Joe called again, "have you got the flu?"

The door opened wider and there she was. She stood in the doorway looking at them both with her bright, black eyes. "No, I haven't got the flu," she said. "I'm just not up to much." She came out slowly and stood on the steps of the roundabout.

"I thought you was some more of those folks from the Council poking around," she said. "They make me ill, they do. Always talking rubbish." She patted the tail of the spotted horse. "We ain't going nowhere, Dukie, are we?" she said.

Joe looked at his father.

"Hullo, Mrs Peg," said Joe's father. "I'm Toni from the café. I'm Joe's father. We read in the paper about the Council buying this land. Didn't they write and tell you about it?"

Granny Peg looked at him. She went into the roundabout and came back with a tin box full of letters. She handed them to Joe's father. "You have a look," she said.

Joe's father took the letters. "But

you haven't opened them," he said.

"What use would that be," said Granny Peg, "seeing as how I can't read them?"

"You need some glasses," said Joe.

Granny Peg shook her head. "My eyes are as sharp as ever they were," she said. "I just never did learn to read."

"Why not?" asked Joe.

"I suppose I was never in school long enough," she said.

Joe's father was looking through the letters. "I'm afraid you should have got someone to read these for you," he said. "It looks to me as though the Council have bought this bit of land and you will have to move."

"Well, I won't!" said Granny Peg

sharply. "This is my home and I'm staying here." She got up stiffly. "You can take the letters if you like. They're no use to me. Now I'm tired. I'm off for my forty winks." She did look tired and very small, thought Joe.

"I'll send Joe round with some food for you tomorrow," said his father. "Some of my soup. That will cheer you up, eh?"

"Please yourself," she said and closed the door.

Chapter Seven

The next day and the day after, and all that week, Joe took Granny Peg food from the café. One day it was soup, another day a nice piece of chicken, another day a pizza. She wasn't very keen on the pizza. Each day they had a chat but Joe could see that Granny Peg was unhappy.

When he went on Friday she was very cross. She was banging about with a broom, sweeping down her steps.

"I told her," she shouted, when she saw Joe.

"Told who?" he asked.

"That young woman!" she cried. "I told her—get off my steps and never come back again. I've had hundreds of children on this roundabout, hundreds. But I don't want you putting your foot on it. I told her."

"Who was she?" asked Joe.

"Some busybody from the Council," said Granny Peg. "Telling me she'd found me another home. Now, Mrs Peg, she said. It's a very nice, comfortable home, she said. You'll like it, she said. How does she know what I'd like?" Granny Peg glared at Joe. "She never had her head in the clouds, never!" She looked at Joe for a moment. "Not like you and me, Joe, eh?" she said softly. She smiled at him. Her old black eyes shone.

She didn't need to speak another word. Joe knew. Together they climbed up onto the roundabout. Together they closed their eyes and the magic began. First the music, very faint but getting clearer. Then the moving, slowly, oh so slowly at first. Just one turn and then another. Then faster and faster. Joe felt again the rush of the wind on his face. He heard the neighing of his horse and he was filled with a wild happiness. Joe and Granny Peg held hands and he heard her singing. He wished it could go on for ever but he knew it couldn't. Sure enough, they began to slow down, down, down. The music faded away and they were still. Joe opened his eyes.

Granny Peg was looking at him. "That was what I needed," she said. "Just one more ride on the roundabout." She climbed down. She patted the horse. "Dear old Dukie," she said, "you're my good old friend." They went into the roundabout.

"Shall I make you a cup of tea?" asked Joe.

Granny Peg shook her head. "No, no thank you, Joe," she said. "I'm tired. You know, Joe, I've had such a good, long life. I've done all my exploring now but you, you've got all yours to do. Don't you forget that, Joe, will you?" She smiled at him. "Goodbye, Joe," she said. "Close the door after you."

The next day, Joe was too busy to go to the roundabout. Some friends of his father's had booked the whole café for a party. Joe had to help his father put up extra tables and tie balloons and paper chains across the ceiling.

"Whose birthday is it?" asked Joe.

"Nobody's," said his father. "It's an engagement party—when somebody decides to get married."

"I'm never going to get married," said Joe. "I'm going to be an explorer."

"Perhaps you might marry another explorer," said his mother.

"Girls can't be explorers, can they?" asked Joe.

"Of course they can," said his mother. "If they don't have to work

all day in a café, that is." Joe's father laughed.

It was a great party. Everyone sang and danced and had fun. Joe was allowed to stay up until the end. He thought that getting married couldn't be too bad. Everyone had been so happy.

He was so tired he slept until after eleven. Crikey! he thought when he looked at his clock, it's nearly afternoon. I've nearly missed this morning. He went downstairs. His mother and father had gone a long time ago. Joe sat drinking orange juice and yawning. He washed himself very slowly and pulled on his jeans and his tee-shirt. Then he went to the café to see what his father would give him to take to Granny Peg.

Joe left the café with some slices of turkey and a big piece of cake left over from the party. He walked slowly. He was still tired. It was a cloudy morning and looked as though it might rain. As he pushed his way through the bushes by the roundabout, Joe heard voices. He ran towards them. If it was someone else from the Council, Granny Peg would get cross. He'd better hurry.

There was a man on the steps of the roundabout and another walking away towards the water tap. The door was open. The man on the steps turned and Joe saw that he was a policeman.

"Hello, sonny." He smiled at Joe.

"Where's Granny Peg?" asked Joe.

"I'm afraid—" said the policeman,

then stopped. "Was she your granny?" he asked.

"No, she's my friend," said Joe. "I've brought her her dinner. Look." He showed the policeman the parcel.

The policeman looked sad. "I'm afraid she won't be needing any dinner," he said, softly. "What's your name, sonny?"

"Joe," whispered Joe.

"Well, Joe." The policeman closed the door into the roundabout and came down the steps. He put his hand on Joe's shoulder. "Mrs Peg died in her sleep," he said. "She just went to sleep and never woke up again."

Joe felt a cold, hard lump of sadness fix itself inside his chest. He knew people died. He knew nobody lived for ever. He was nearly eight years old and he knew that. He just couldn't believe that he would never see Granny Peg again. He looked at the parcel of food and his eyes filled with tears. He didn't want the policeman to see him cry. He threw the food into the bushes and ran back the way he had come.

He sat down on the bank by the spiders' web until he had finished crying. Then he wiped his eyes and blew his nose and walked back to the café. But as soon as he saw his dad his eyes filled up with tears again.

When he told his mother and father what had happened they sat him down in the kitchen. "Now, you just eat this and you listen to me," said his father, putting him out a big

bowl of spaghetti with Joe's favourite sauce. "Of course you are sad. But you are sad for yourself. You mustn't be sad for Granny Peg. She was very old and very tired."

Joe's mother put her arm around him. "And remember, Joe," she said, "Granny Peg didn't want to move. She wanted to stay in the roundabout for the rest of her life, didn't she?"

Joe nodded. "But I just didn't know she had such a little bit of life left," he said. The sad feeling in his chest was still there but it wasn't as bad as before. He felt very tired.

Chapter Eight

On Monday morning, a letter
plopped through the letter box. Joe

picked it up. "It's from Italy!" he
said. He recognized the stamp and

his granny's writing.

His father sat down to read it and smiled. "Well, well, Joe," he said, "you're in luck. Your granny's won some money and she wants to buy you a plane ticket to go and see her. How about that?"

Joe's eyes opened wide. "All by myself?" he said.

"Why not?" asked his father. "It will be an adventure. It'll be like exploring, won't it?"

Joe thought about it. Somehow he didn't quite feel like exploring at the moment. He still felt very sad. But he would like to see his real granny again.

"You'll have a lovely time," said his mother. "You'll be able to go to the beach with your cousins and you'll learn some more Italian, too."

Joe already knew a few words. His granny had talked to him often in Italian but he had forgotten lots of it.

"How many cousins have I got?" he asked.

"Three," said his father. "We'll go to buy the ticket as soon as we can. You'll have a wonderful holiday. I wish I was coming."

Joe began to cheer up.

By the time the day came to go to Italy, he was very excited. His father took him to the airport. There were three other children travelling alone on the same plane. Joe sat with them and waved to his father.

When the plane took off, for a moment it reminded him of the roundabout. He felt the sadness again but then he looked down and

saw the fields beneath him and soon he saw the edge of the land and the

beginning of the sea. It was like
looking at a giant map and Joe loved
maps.

Joe's granny was at the airport to
meet him and so were his uncle and
his three cousins. Carlo was ten,

Elena was seven and little Marco was
four. They all talked at once as they
carried his bags to the car. It was

very hot and sunny in Italy.

They all lived together in a house not far from the sea. Every day they went to the beach. Joe was very happy. There were so many new things to see. His granny was so pleased to see him. She cooked him mountains of spaghetti and she was always giving him peaches and grapes to eat. Every evening, after supper they would go for a walk into the town and eat wonderful ice-creams. Joe found that he remembered lots of Italian words.

His granny was brown from the sun and her legs were better. She asked him all about his father and mother and how the café was doing. Joe was going to tell her about Granny Peg but he didn't. He was

having such a great time he didn't want to remember how sad he had been. He went exploring with Carlo and Elena. "When we're grown up we're going exploring all over the world together," he told his granny.

At last the holiday was over. The whole family came to the airport to see him off. His cousins promised to write. Carlo was going to start learning English when he went back to school. "Next time you come you must bring your father and mother and your Auntie Nina," said his granny. She loaded him up with bags of fruit and special cakes she had

made for his father. She waved and waved until the plane took off and Joe flew back to England.

Joe's mother and father met him at the airport. They hugged and kissed him and his father was very pleased when he saw the special cakes Granny had made. "My favourites!" he cried.

"You've grown, Joe," said his mother, "and look how brown you are. Did you have a lovely time?"

"Brilliant!" said Joe. "Can I go again next year?"

"We'll see," said his mother.

For the next few days Joe felt very dreary. It seemed cold in England. "You always feel like that after a holiday," said his father. "Cheer up. You'll be going back to school next week."

On the last day of the holidays Joe's mother took him to buy some new clothes. They went by bus and after they had finished shopping they had some tea and cakes in a café. His mother enjoyed that. "It makes a change for me to be waited on," she said. Joe was feeling pleased because he had new trainers, a new anorak and two new pullovers.

"It must have been all the food that Gran gave me that made me grow out of my clothes," he said.

On the way home, Joe was looking out of the bus window when he suddenly recognized the road they were in. There was the high fence covered with posters. The bus slowed down just by the little door. He saw a man coming through it

wearing a yellow helmet. Over the
top of the fence he could see a crane
moving and the top of a bulldozer.
Joe slid right down in his seat. He

didn't want to look. There was just a
little piece of sadness still inside him
somewhere.

On Monday he started in the
Juniors. He felt very grown up. The

Juniors was in a different building from the Infants. It was much bigger and had its own playground. Joe's new teacher was called Mr Cole. Joe knew straight away that he was going to like him. As soon as he walked into the classroom he was quite sure.

All the walls were covered with maps and pictures of interesting places. There were pictures of Eskimos fishing through holes in the ice. There were people growing bananas and pineapples. There were mountains and rivers with crocodiles. Mr Cole had a cupboard with glass doors which was filled with the strangest things. He even had an ostrich egg. The biggest egg Joe had ever seen. Joe was very happy in his new class and the weeks flew by.

Chapter Nine

One day when Joe came home from school, his father was looking very worried. "We've got to look for another café," he said.

"Why?" asked Joe. "What's wrong with this one?"

"It's being sold," said his father. "I'd really like somewhere bigger but I'm not sure if I can find anywhere." He scratched his head and sighed. "Just when we're so busy," he said.

For the next few weeks Joe's father was always rushing off to look at places but one day he came back looking much more cheerful.

"You've found somewhere?" asked Joe.

His father nodded. "We'll be moving the week before Christmas," he said. "It's brand new, not quite finished yet."

"Is it far away?" asked Joe.

"Not too far," said his father. "It's bigger than here. We can have four or five more tables and you should see the kitchen. Things are looking up, Joe."

Joe was pleased. "If we make a lot of money can we all go to Italy next year?" he asked. His father laughed. "I'm not promising."

Joe was looking forward to Christmas. His father was going to buy him a bicycle. When the time for moving came, all Joe's father's friends came to help him. Joe wanted to help, too, but his parents wouldn't let him. "No, Joe," they said, "we want it to be a surprise. Wait until it's all ready."

Joe could see that they were both very excited about the new place.

On the last day of the Christmas term, his father picked him up from school.

"Today," he said, "you shall have your tea in the smartest place in town." His eyes were shining. Joe was excited. At last he was going to see the new café. They drove through the streets. It was almost dark. People were hurrying home carrying their Christmas shopping. Joe's father turned and stopped the car outside the back of a new building. It was cold and Joe shivered as he got out of the warm car.

They went through the back door and down a passage. Joe's father opened the door into the kitchen. Auntie Nina was there and his mother. Everything was gleaming new and it was twice as big as the old kitchen.

"Wow! Fantastic!" said Joe. "You'll be able to cook piles of food in here. Gosh, I'm starving." He sat down in the brand new kitchen and started on a piece of chocolate cake.

Suddenly he stopped eating. A strange feeling came over him. He thought he could hear music. It was special, old-fashioned music. He had

heard that music before. But it couldn't be. He looked at his father. He didn't know what to say.

His father smiled. "Come on, Joe," he said. "You haven't seen the rest of the café yet."

As Joe followed his father through the door, the music got louder. He walked between the new tables with their red cloths as if he was in a dream. He could see something wonderful outside the window of his dad's new café. Something round and coloured with twisting golden poles.

"It's a roundabout!" he shouted. "It's Granny Peg's roundabout!"

Joe's father took him outside to meet the man who had bought the roundabout. He told Joe how he

loved old roundabouts. He showed him that he had repainted every inch. Dukie had bright new spots. Georgie the giraffe looked splendid. The whole roundabout gleamed and sparkled. The machinery was cleaned and oiled. Joe watched the wheels and cogs all turning. "This new shopping centre is called the Roundabout Centre," said his father. "It was built on the waste ground where Granny Peg used to live."

Joe watched the children riding the roundabout. They hung onto the animals and laughed and waved. He knew that they would never have a ride as wonderful as those he'd had with Granny Peg. But he looked at their happy faces and knew that she would have been very glad.

He would never forget her, the old woman who lived in the roundabout. He remembered what she had said the last time he saw her. "You've got all your exploring to do, Joe," she had said and she was right. As he listened to the music and watched the roundabout turning, Joe felt the last little corner of sadness in his heart melt away.

"Come on, Joe," said his father. "Let's switch on the lights in our new café and wait for the first customers, eh?"

STREAMERS

We've got lots of great books for younger readers in Hippo's STREAMERS series:

Broomstick Services by Ann Jungman £1.75
When Joe, Lucy and Jackie find two witches sleeping in the school caretaker's shed, they can't believe their eyes. When they hear that the witches want to be ordinary, they can't believe their ears. But they help the witches set up *Broomstick Services* and then the fun really begins . . .

Paws – A Panda Full of Surprises
by Joan Stimson £1.75
Every year Uncle Cyril sends Trevor an exciting birthday present. But this year he seems to have forgotten. That is until a smart delivery truck arrives outside Trevor's house bringing the most fantastic present Trevor could ever have dreamed of – Paws!

Aristotle Sludge by Margaret Leroy £1.75
Class 1C's routing changes completely when Aristotle Sludge explodes into their lives. Looking after a baby dinosaur means a lot of hard work – but with Aristotle Sludge around there's a lot of fun too!

The Old Woman Who Lived In A Roundabout
by Ruth Silvestre £1.75
When Joe discovers a roundabout whilst out exploring, he can hardly believe his eyes. And when he finds out that an old woman lives in it, he is truly amazed. But, before long Joe and Granny Peg become firm friends and magical things begin to happen . . .

Look out for these other titles in the STREAMERS series:

Nate the Great by Marjorie Sharmat
Nate the Great and the Missing Key by Marjorie Sharmat
Sally Ann – On Her Own by Terrance Dicks
Sally Ann – The School Play by Terrance Dicks
Sally Ann – The Picnic by Terrance Dicks
Sally Ann – Goes to Hospital by Terrance Dicks
The Little Yellow Taxi and His Friends by Ruth Ainsworth

HIPPO BESTSELLERS

Indiana Jones And The Last Crusade (story book) by Anne Digby	£2.95
Marlene Marlow Investigates The Great Christmas Pudding Mystery (fiction) by Roy Apps	£1.75
Marlene Marlow Investigates The Missing Tapes Affair (fiction) by Roy Apps	£1.75
Swimming Club No 1: Splashdown (fiction) by Micheal Hardcastle	£1.75
Swimming Club No 2: Jump In (fiction) by Micheal Hardcastle	£1.75
Beware This House is Haunted (fiction) by Lance Salway	£1.95
The Plonkers Handbook (humour) by Charles Alverson	£1.95
Knock Knock Joke Book by Scouler Anderson	£1.95
Coping With Parents (humour) by Peter Corey	£1.95
Private Lives (non-fiction) by Melvyn Bagnall	£2.50
The Spooky Activity Book by Karen King	£2.25
Christmas Fun (activity) by Karen King	£2.25